My
Second Best
Friend

Also by Geraldine Kaye in Scholastic Press:

The Dragon Upstairs

Geraldine Kaye

SCHOLASTIC
PRESS

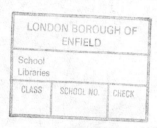
Scholastic Children's Books,
Commonwealth House, 1–19 New Oxford Street
London WC1A 1NU, UK
a division of Scholastic Ltd
London ~ New York ~ Toronto ~ Sydney ~ Auckland

First published by Scholastic Ltd, 1998

ISBN 0 590 54324 5

Typeset by DP Photosetting, Aylesbury, Bucks
Printed by Cox & Wyman Ltd, Reading, Berks

10 9 8 7 6 5 4 3 2

Chapter One

It was dark when Lucy woke: probably the middle of the night, because she couldn't hear the telly downstairs. A loud noise had woken her but she couldn't hear it now. Perhaps she had just had a loud noisy dream? Lucy turned over and Rosabel fell on the floor.

Lucy was almost asleep when she heard the noise again, a rumbling-tumbling noise. It was coming from the plot next door which had a tall hedge all round it.

The plot used to be *their* garden and last summer she and her best friend Polly had slept there in a tent, which was ace. But then Dad sold it to Mr Tolley to build a bungalow. Mr and Mrs Tolley came at weekends and he put big flat stones down on the lawn, "making a terrace", he said, and Mrs Tolley planted bulbs "ready for the spring" and Dad put a line of baby evergreens so he wouldn't have to look at the Tolley's bungalow for the rest of his life. But surely nobody would start building a bungalow in the middle of the night?

Footsteps. Lucy looked out of the window. The moon was pale and thin like a slice of melon and a man was standing on Mr Tolley's terrace and beckoning towards the road.

"Come on, Reub," he whispered and his

voice was quite loud and sort of rusty. "Bit of 'ard standin', innit?"

Lucy wasn't frightened but she was mystified. *Mystified* had been her favourite word since Miss Wells put it on the blackboard for the spelling test the week before last. Suddenly she saw two big white eyes coming through the gap in the hedge. The eyes were bumping and thumping towards her and almost at once she knew they were the headlights of a lorry crossing the pavement and the rumbling-tumbling was the trailer behind it. The lorry pulled the trailer right on to Mr Tolley's terrace and then stopped. The headlights went out and people jumped down and went into the trailer.

"Wicked!" Lucy whispered. *Wicked* was her other favourite word. Lucy loved trailers and caravans. They had stayed in one every summer before the twins were born. She went on watching but she could only see shadows behind the curtains and a flickery gaslight. Then the light went out and Lucy slept.

It was Sunday when she woke, bells were ringing far away. The lorry and the trailer were still there and a grey dog wandered about dragging a bit of chain. The lorry was old and battered and the trailer was quite different from the ones Lucy had stayed in. It was white and patterned all over with bits of silvery metal and, besides, it had a chimney.

Suddenly the man and boy opened the door and jumped down.

"Off out," the man shouted. He wore a black jacket and a red kerchief round his neck. The boy had a black cowboy hat with a white fringe round the brim. He looked about twelve, Lucy thought, but hadn't he driven the lorry on to the plot? Fancy driving a lorry and trailer when you were twelve.

The boy tied the dog to the wheel of the trailer and the man unhitched the lorry and they drove off.

Lucy went on watching. What was the trailer doing there anyway? How long was it stopping? Inside she could see a girl with long dark hair and a red dress. The girl was tying holly into bundles with string. Her mother was washing-up at the sink. It was like watching people in a play, Lucy thought. She was a shepherd in the Christmas play at school next week.

"Breakfast, Lucy!" Dad called, knocking at her bedroom door.

"Coming!" She jumped out of bed. She wouldn't say anything about the trailer. Much better not. Dad and Mum might not even notice because most of the house windows looked the other way. If she told them they might *do* something. Anyway, it was her secret.

"Cornflakes or crispies?" Mum said. The twins, Danny and Davy, were already sitting at the table and Mum had a teaspoon in either hand. "Come along, Danny, one for Mummy."

"Shan't," Danny said, pushing the spoon away.

"Why can't we have egg and bacon on Sunday like we always used to?" Lucy said.

"I really haven't got time to cook breakfast in the morning with the twins and everything to see to," Mum said. "Come along, Davy, one for Daddy."

"Maybe Lucy and me could cook egg and bacon *next* Sunday?" Dad said.

"Fine," Mum said, and turned to smile encouragingly just as Danny knocked his orange juice over.

"Oh, Danny!" Mum cried. "Get a paper towel will you, Lucy?"

"Messy little boy," Lucy said, mopping up orange.

"Not messy," Danny said.

"I'm a big boy now," Davy said.

"Not too big to go in my bedroom yesterday and scribble on my wall," Lucy said.

"Didn't," Danny and Davy said together.

"Oh, dear!" Mum said. "But if you remembered to shut your bedroom door, Lucy, they couldn't get in. You were just as bad at two years old, worse in fact."

"That's not fair," Lucy said. "Anyway, they can reach the door handle now."

"Maybe I could put a bolt high up or a hook?" Dad said.

After breakfast Lucy put on her anorak, fetched Rosabel and went outside. The new fence looked yellow in the winter sun. The girl and the mother in the trailer were both tying holly in bundles and presently the mother stood up. She was very fat, as fat as Mum had been before the twins were born.

Ma pulled a shawl round herself and picked up the basket.

"Off out, Bel," she said. "Old dog's tied up, innit. Don't open no door to no *gavvers* nor nobody."

"Course not," Bel said. It was warm with the gas stove but cold air rushed in as Ma opened the door and then slammed it shut. Bel watched as she disappeared through the gap in the tall hedge on to the pavement.

Bel looked at the fence and the house next door. Left on her own she was a bit scared of "house people" and didn't like stopping in towns much. Summertime was best. Summertime was bean-picking and strawberry-picking for her and Ma and gate-mending and scrap-dealing for Reuben and Pa and they stopped on farms and woods where everything was quiet and green instead of noisy lay-bys and empty plots.

Bel saw something then. A girl was looking at her over the fence, a house girl with blue eyes. She was holding up a doll with gold hair and a pink dress all pretty and sparkly. Bel's own doll had lost one eye and its dress was ragged. The house girl smiled and climbed on to the fence but the dog jumped out on his chain barking and she jumped back. Fancy being scared of Rover, Bel thought. She wasn't scared of any old dog.

"Shut it," she shouted. She came out of the trailer then. She wanted to see the gold-haired doll close to. Had to. She jerked Rover's chain and he slunk to his box growling.

"What ye want then?" Bel said looking at Lucy.

"Nothing. Just looking at your trailer," Lucy said.

"Got yer eyeful then?" Bel said.

"Are you ... are you a Gypsy?" Lucy said.

"Who ye calling *Gypsy*? Travellers us, not didicois nor nothing, Romanys. Never stop anywhere long."

"Oh," Lucy said. "Well, I'm just plain English but my granny's from Scotland and I really love caravans. Can I . . . I mean can I look inside yours, please?"

"What?" Bel blinked. Most house people hated caravans. "What for?"

"Just to see," Lucy said.

Bel thought for a minute. "If ye let us 'old yer doll, ye can come inside," she said. "Right?"

"Right," Lucy said, climbing over the fence.

"Shut it," Bel shouted as Rover jumped out barking again. "Shut it, ye varmint."

Bel opened the door with one hand and held out the other for the doll.

"She's called Rosabel." Lucy stepped up into the trailer and gazed round. It wasn't like any trailer she had seen except for the Calor gas. It was bigger and there were shiny red seats which turned into beds and red satin cushions trimmed with lace, paper flowers and two large stainless-steel bowls hanging from two hooks like silver moons and photographs of weddings and blue and gold china, Crown Derby, her granny had a plate like that, along one shelf beside three cut-glass bowls and a bucket full of empty tins and a shower at one end and a television set at the other.

"Wicked!" Lucy breathed.

"Kushti!" Bel whispered, fingering the doll's pink dress. "She's Rosabel and I'm Bel for Isabel, funny innit?"

"Kushti would be a nice name, Kushti

Rosabel," Lucy said dreamily. "Must be lovely living in a trailer? How long you stopping?"

"Never stop anywhere long," Bel said.

"Do you go to school?"

"Course. Sometimes. Been to lots of schools. Hundreds."

"You could come to our school. Crossroads School. Miss Wells is quite nice. So is Mrs Budd."

Bel shook her head. "Just come 'ere for the 'ospital. Ma's got this baby coming..."

Chapter Two

As soon as Lucy woke on Monday she sat up and looked out of the window. The lorry and trailer were still there and so far Dad and Mum hadn't even noticed. Fancy not even noticing a trailer parked next door. Lucy dressed for school and then rolled her dressing-gown small and pushed it down in her school bag. "Don't forget to bring your dressing-gowns," Miss Wells had said on Friday afternoon. "And we need a doll for baby Jesus, so if you've got a really nice baby doll bring that too. And don't anybody *dare* go down with this tummy-bug that's going round!" Miss Wells pretended to look fierce and everybody laughed.

Lucy's dressing-gown was a bit small but Mum didn't have time for dressing-gown shopping these days because of the twins. Kushti Rosabel was pretty but she wasn't a baby doll. Polly was lucky, she was Mary in the school play *and* she had a really nice baby doll. It wouldn't be fair if Polly's doll was baby Jesus in the Christmas play as well.

Lucy fetched a bandage from the bathroom cupboard and tied it tight round Kushti Rosabel's head and tried to pull a bonnet over it. But she still didn't look like a baby doll.

"Stupid!" Lucy said and went down to breakfast.

"Morning, Lucy dear," Mum said. She had a spoon in either hand. "One for Mummy, Davy?" Dad had already left for work.

"Lucy feed Davy?" Davy said, grabbing at the spoon and scattering cornflakes everywhere.

"No thanks," Lucy said. "Big boys feed themselves."

"He's got a cold, poor mite," Mum said.

"Off out," Pa said, jumping down from the trailer. He and Reuben drove off in the lorry.

Bel sat at the table tying holly into bundles but she watched the pavement through the gap in the tall hedge too.

Children were walking to school and they all seemed to be carrying things like woolly sheep or baby dolls. Funny sort of school, Bel thought. School was for pencils and writing, not woolly sheep and baby dolls.

"Off out." Ma pulled her shawl round her shoulders and picked up the basket. "Gotta sell all this quick afore they red berries drop off. Can't sell 'olly without red berries. Ye coming, Bel?"

"Yeah," Bel said. It was warm inside and outside the grass was all sugary with frost and the sky was dark as a pond. But Bel didn't want to stop in the trailer by herself all day. She pulled her anorak over her dress. "Age 11 to 12" it said on the label and Bel was nine and small for her age.

"Bit of 'ard standing, innit?" Ma said, poking Mr Tolley's terrace with her foot as Bel jumped down after her.

"Buy my bunch of 'olly, lady," Ma said as they got to the pavement. She used a special wheedling voice for selling. "Lovely bit of 'olly, sir. Look at they red berries. Ye got a lucky face."

Some people bought holly, others just walked on. Bel watched and wondered if she would ever sell holly as well as Ma. Ma wasn't scared of anybody.

"Try over 'ere, Bel," Ma said, pointing across the road. "And don't talk to no gavvers."

Bel took two bundles and crossed. The pavements were quiet now, children already in school, grown-up people in their shops or offices.

"Buy my 'olly, lady, lovely bit of 'olly," Bel whispered.

"Where did it come from I wonder?" the lady said, walking on. People didn't say things like that to Ma.

"Come from the country," Bel murmured, thinking of green woods. She wandered along the pavement. There were railings and a notice and she could hear singing. She knew that song from the school in Yate last Christmas. *While Shepherds Washed*, was that it? Bel stopped and spelled the notice out loud.

"C-r-o-s-s-r-o-a-d-s." She knew the other word was *School*. "Crossroads School," she said and it was just by a crossroads. Ma and Pa had never been to school and Reuben only went for a week and didn't take to it. But Bel liked school.

The singing finished and now she could hear chatter and the scrape of chairs. She crept across the playground and looked in.

It wasn't like an ordinary classroom with tables and chairs and children in bluebell-blue like the school in Yate or holly-green like the school at Taunton. The tables and chairs had been pushed to one side and some children wore white nightgowns and silver wings and some wore dressing-gowns back-to-front with tea-cloths tied on their heads and woolly sheep or baby dolls under their arms. Bel frowned. Didn't they do reading and writing at this no-good school?

Then Bel saw Lucy. She didn't know her at first in her back-to-front dressing-gown. But Lucy knew Bel and she waved and children came to the window. For a moment the whole class stared out and Bel stared in. Then suddenly Miss Wells came out to the playground and Lucy followed.

"You're from a travelling family, aren't you? What's your name?" Miss Wells asked. "Do you want to come to school?"

Bel turned and ran back to the pavement then but Lucy ran out after her.

"Miss Wells says I've got to take you to Mrs Budd," she panted, out of breath.

"What?" Bel said. She wasn't sure about Miss Wells and Mrs Budd but it was cold stuck out on the pavement and lonely too. She followed Lucy in and down the corridor.

"Thank you, Lucy," Mrs Budd said, smiling and shuffling papers. "Sit down, Bel. Have you been to school before?"

"Course," Bel said. Her heart was thumping. "Lots."

"Which schools?"

"Temple Cloud, Redhill, school in a bus ... can't remember."

"Well, that's a start," Mrs Budd said, handing her a pencil. "Will you write your name for me, please?"

"Course," Bel said, and curled her tongue over her lip and wrote *Bel Lovell* in big spidery letters, though she hadn't been to school for a month.

"Good," Mrs Budd said. "How long are you stopping here?"

"Never stop anywhere long," Bel said.

"Would Mother or Father come and see me, do you think?" Mrs Budd said, but Bel shook her head. "Oh well, I think we'll try you in Miss Wells' class for today. Come along."

Mrs Budd didn't seem surprised to find

everybody in the class in nightgowns and wings or back-to-front dressing-gowns. "We have a new pupil today, children, Bel Lovell."

"Hello, Bel Lovell. Welcome to Crossroads School," the class chanted. Everybody stared at Bel and Bel stared back. Mrs Budd whispered to Miss Wells for a minute and then left.

Lucy's hand waved in the air. "Please can Bel be a shepherd in the play with me? I promise I'll look after her."

"But Gypsies can't read nor nothing," Ben said. "Bet she hasn't got a dressing-gown."

"Who ye calling *Gypsy*?" Bel muttered. "Romanys we are, Romany travellers." Ma would think she'd gone back to the trailer, wouldn't she?

"I think Bel had better just watch the rehearsal today," Miss Wells said. "See how things go."

The buzzer went then and everybody took off their back-to-front dressing-gowns and Lucy and Polly took Bel to dinner which was toad-in-the-hole and carrots and jam-roll. After that they went out to play. Bel didn't know hopscotch or skipping and she did know it was better not to say where she had come from or where she was going to either.

Presently the buzzer went again and everybody ran inside and put on their back-to-front dressing-gowns and went to the hall ready for rehearsal. There were two big green curtains and footlights in front of the stage. Bel stared at the green curtains but she didn't like being inside much. She liked the sky above her head.

"More changes, I'm afraid," Miss Wells said. "Kate and Don have gone home like Jack and John did on Friday."

"The tummy-bug, wasn't it," Jack said. "I was sick all night."

"Poor you," Miss Wells said. "Anyway, we've got to get on. So Adil, will you be a shepherd today and Kylie, will you be an angel?"

Sharon's hand waved in the air. "Jordan was sick after dinner. He's gone home too."

"Oh, dear," Miss Wells said. "Looks like we need spares for all the parts in the play. Please, please, don't anybody else get sick before Thursday, the big day when the Lord Mayor's coming."

"I'm all right," said Polly and Lynton at the same time. Polly was Mary of course and Lynton was Joseph.

"Excellent," Miss Wells said. "Now first I want to choose a doll for Jesus. Bring your baby dolls up here, will you?"

Polly and Kylie and Sharon had all brought baby dolls.

"Only three?" Miss Wells said.

"Kate brought her doll today but she took it home again when she got sick," Polly said.

"Oh dear!" Miss Wells said. "Now let me look." She looked at each doll carefully and then said, "I think this is the one for baby Jesus."

"That's my one," Polly said and smiled and carried the baby doll to the manger.

"Thank you, Polly," Miss Wells said.

"That's not fair," Lucy whispered to herself but she didn't really mind that much now Bel was there.

"Let's get on with our rehearsal," Miss Wells said. "Ready with the curtains, Paul and Saul?"

"Do you know the story about Jesus and Bethlehem?" Lucy whispered helpfully as Bel sat down to watch.

"Course," Bel said. "Born in a manger."

Bel stared at the curtains. It was like the country, all that green, and first Mary was there with an angel and then two boys pulled the green curtains back and Joseph was there too with a grey woolly donkey which was really a grey woolly donkey costume with Ben and Jack inside. Bel liked the donkey and laughed when it jumped and kicked. But Miss Wells got cross.

Bel heard Lucy and the other shepherds say their words: "Look at that bright star!" and later on, "I bring this gift for baby Jesus," and she heard the kings' words too. She had never seen a play before and her dark eyes shone. When everybody sang *While Shepherds Watched*, Bel sang too.

"Look, the Gypsy girl's singing," Kylie whispered.

"Why shouldn't she?" Lucy and Polly said together and then Lucy added, "She's been to school, lots of schools."

"Goodbye, everybody," Miss Wells said when the buzzer went. "See you tomorrow and no more you-know-what, please."

Lucy and Polly and Bel walked slowly down the road. Polly's house was first. "Goodbye then," Polly said.

Lights were already on in the trailer and it looked quite cosy and Rover jumped out of his box but he didn't bark.

"You coming to school tomorrow?" Lucy asked.

"Course," said Bel.

Chapter Three

"Going to school again, Bel?" Ma said on Tuesday morning. Pa and Reuben had already driven off in the lorry.

"Course," Bel said.

"Learning yer books? Learning yer writing?" Ma said hopefully. Ma knew about numbers and prices but reading and writing was a puzzle. Reuben had been to school for a week once but he wouldn't go again whatever she said and it was too late now. Reuben worked with Pa, her Reuby did a grown man's work at twelve years old and walked with a proper Gypsy man's swagger. Reuby was all right, Ma thought, but she was glad that Bel was going to school, had taken to it like a duck to water.

"Course," said Bel.

"Going off like that," Ma said. "Worried sick, wasn't I? Ye tell us if ye want to go to school."

"Course," said Bel. She had liked watching the Christmas play. She would like being in it even more. She wasn't that good at reading and writing but she could dance and twirl like a leaf and sing like a nightingale. She would show everybody at Crossroads School, course she would.

"Plait yer hair, shall I?" Ma looked round for the comb to start the long, painful business of combing through the tangles.

"Course," Bel said, scowling at the comb. Lots of girls at Crossroads School had plaits. Polly's were long and fair and Charlene had a dozen little plaits all over her head.

Half an hour later, hair neatly plaited, Bel walked out to the pavement. She paused a moment outside Lucy's house but she didn't dare knock at the door. Maybe Lucy had gone to school already? Bel walked on to Crossroads School playground.

"Look who's here!" Ben said loudly.

"Gypsy girl, innit," Kylie said. Behind her Adil and Femi smiled and tried not to look worried. Bel frowned, but her heart was thudding. A circle of children came round her but Lucy wasn't in the playground, nor was Polly.

"Who ye calling Gypsy?"

"Gyppo then, that better?" Ben said.

"My mum says Gypsies are dirty," Sharon said, wrinkling her nose. "My mum says they shouldn't let Gypsies in our school because of nits. She's going to write."

" '*My mother said that I never should*

  Play with the Gypsies in the wood,' " Kylie sang, but suddenly she saw Miss Wells at the classroom window and stopped in the middle of the verse.

"That's not fair, three against one!" Lucy said, arriving with Polly just then. "That's mean, that is. Anyway, you had nits the term before last."

"So did you," Sharon said.

"Everybody in Crossroads School had nits the term before last," Polly said, flicking her plaits behind her shoulders. She hated teasing and quarrelling and always kept the peace if she could.

"I didn't," Jack said. "I never had one nit in my whole life." Just then the buzzer went and Lucy and Polly got into line with Bel between them.

"Shall I knock at the trailer door for you tomorrow?" Lucy whispered as they filed inside. Long as Mum and Dad didn't notice the trailer, she thought. Maybe they wouldn't, because Dad went off to work early and Mum was busy getting fussed about the twins' colds.

"Course," said Bel.

In the hall the curtains were closed for assembly behind Mrs Budd and the whole school was there. Bel kept her eyes on the green curtains, green was safe, but she felt all shivery-quivery. She didn't like being stuck inside with so many house people like a rabbit in a hutch. Summertime was best. Greentime. Spring came first, Pa said spring was when you could put your foot on twelve daisies. June they would go to Appleby Fair for the horses and weddings.

"Anybody else away today?" Miss Wells said when they got back to the classroom.

"Kate and Don and Jordan aren't back yet," Polly said.

"Please, Miss, Kamal isn't coming to school today. His mum phoned the office."

"Oh dear, Kamal and Jordan are both kings," Miss Wells said and as Lucy's hand waved in the air she added, "Yes, Lucy?"

"If Kate's still away, can Bel be a shepherd today?"

"Don't want no Gypsies in our Christmas play," Kylie muttered.

"Bet she can't even read," Ben said.

"That's quite enough of that," Miss Wells said firmly. "Before we get on with our first lesson there are one or two things I want to say. Sit down, everybody." Chair legs scraped the floor and everybody sat. Miss Wells took a map from the cupboard and hooked it over the blackboard.

"Who can tell me what this is?" Several hands went up. "Yes, Kylie?"

"It's a map of the whole world, Miss." Bel blinked and stared, she had never seen a map of the whole world.

"Good," Miss Wells said, pointing with her ruler. "And who can tell me what this is? Yes, Ben?"

"Great Britain," Ben said.

"Right," Miss Wells said. "Looks quite

small, doesn't it? And what's this? Yes, Sharon?"

"Africa," Sharon said.

"Excellent. East Africa is probably where the first man and woman, the first human beings, started, millions of years ago."

"With the dinosaurs?" Jack said.

"No. After the dinosaurs."

"Femi comes from Africa," Sharon said, and everybody looked at Femi, who looked shyly at the floor. Then Charlene's hand went up.

"My grandma came from Jamaica but my great-great-great-great-great-great-great Grandma came from Africa too," said Charlene, who wasn't at all shy.

"That's right, Charlene," Miss Wells said. "Ever since the beginning people have been travelling about the world settling in different places. The Celts for instance came from Europe and settled all over the British Isles thousands of years ago. Most of us have some Celtic blood and people from Scotland, Ireland and Wales have a lot."

"My granny's Scottish," Lucy whispered.

"My grandad's Irish and my dad and my mum," Kevin said.

"So's mine."

"Hush," Miss Wells said. "The Romans came from Italy down here." The ruler pointed. "After that, Vikings..."

"Proper mongrels, aren't we?" Jack said.

"Yes. But new people bring new ideas and skills and that makes everybody better off," Miss Wells said, and pointed with her ruler. "What country is this?"

"India," Lucy said. "Where Adil's family comes from."

"And Kamal's and Moura's," Polly said.

"And it's where Romany Gypsies came from too," Miss Wells said. "Who knows why they are called Gypsies?"

Silence.

"Can you tell me, Bel?" Bel shook her head.

"Well, they came from Southern India. Romanys were travellers and they started to move round the world about a thousand years ago." Miss Wells pointed with her ruler to the blue Mediterranean sea.

"Some moved this way above the Mediterranean into Europe and others moved that way through Egypt and along the top of Africa. After they left Egypt they were often called 'Egyptians' and that got shortened to Gypsy."

"Did the journey to Europe take a long time?" Adil asked.

"Yes," Miss Wells said. "They took several hundred years to reach England. They were persecuted here at first, accused of stealing babies and bringing the plague because they looked different and spoke their own language."

"Perhaps Gypsies brought the tummy-bug," Jack said but nobody laughed.

"That's not fair," Lucy said. "Anyway you and John and Kate and Don all had the tummy bug *before* the Gypsies came."

"Quite right," Miss Wells said. "And they have a hard time because there aren't enough places for them to stop. Now let's have a quiet moment while you all look at the map and think about what I've told you. Then we'll get on with arithmetic."

Everybody was quiet. Lucy thought about Dad and Mum and the trailer next door and how it wouldn't be at all fair if the twins' colds got worse and Mum couldn't even come to the Christmas play. Kylie thought about the choc bar she would buy after school. Bel gazed at the map. She had never heard of Egypt or India. Did Pa and Ma and Reuby know about Egypt and India, she wondered. Polly thought about how she didn't feel very well.

Miss Price came in with a message.

"Gillian isn't well, I've just phoned her mother."

"Help!" Miss Wells said. "She was an angel."

Adil put up his hand. "Can Bel be second shepherd?"

"Good idea," Miss Wells said.

"But she won't know the words," Kylie said. "She ought to be an angel because they stand round the stable and don't speak."

"Second shepherd sounds like a good idea to me," Miss Wells said firmly. "Do you know the shepherd's words, Bel?"

"Course," Bel said, jumping up. " 'Look at that bright star!' and 'I bring this gift for baby Jesus'."

"Good," Lucy whispered. "Wicked!"

"Excellent," Miss Wells said and a few children clapped and then everybody in the class was clapping. Bel twirled round and round with the excitement of it all.

"Oh dordi, dordi!" Bel said.

Chapter Four

"Can Bel sit by me?" Lucy asked. Now Bel was a shepherd she would come to school every day, she thought, now Bel could be her second-best friend.

Miss Wells gave Bel an exercise book. "Write your name on it, Bel," she said. Bel curled her tongue over her lip and wrote "Bel Lovell" on the front of the book in big spidery writing. Then she opened it and wrote "Bel Lovell" inside and she would have written it again but

Miss Wells gave her some sums to add up.

But Bel was soon tired of holding a pencil and sitting still. In the trailer she could get up and go outside whenever she liked. Bel fidgeted and fidgeted adding up her sums. But she was quick at it and got most of them right.

"Done 'em," she whispered. "What now?"

"Write something in your book," Lucy said. She was a bit stuck with her own long division and Bel kept fidgeting and fidgeting. "Write your news."

"What news?" Bel said.

"Write about where you came from and that," Lucy said. "Write about your Pa and Ma and Reuben and travelling all the time and stopping where you want. You know, like a diary?"

"Course," Bel said. She didn't know what a diary was but she did know travelling people never let on about where they had come from or where they were going to. She curled her tongue over her lip and wrote, "Bel Lovell is me an Reuby is me bruvver an he is telv an Ma is tenty-wun and so is Pa." This took Bel a long time and she fidgeted a lot.

"Finished," she said. "Now what?"

"Write about being a shepherd in the play," Lucy said.

Bel sighed and wrote very slowly, 'I am in skool play. I am sheepid.' Miss Wells came round and put a quick red tick.

The buzzer went for dinner and after that it was playtime and then rehearsal.

"Get into your costumes, everybody," Miss Wells said.

The angels put on their white nightgowns and silver wings and everybody else put on their back-to-front dressing-gowns and tea-cloths over their heads except for the kings who had cardboard crowns covered with golden paper. In five minutes everybody in Miss Wells' class looked just like people from Israel long ago except for the angels. And except for Ben and Jack who looked just like a grey woolly donkey.

Polly's back-to-front dressing-gown was blue and new. Polly was lucky, Lucy thought, because she didn't have any little brothers or sisters and her mum was really into shopping.

"I'm a shepherd," Bel said and turned her too-big anorak back to front and Miss Wells found a spare tea-cloth and a woolly sheep to go under her arm. "Look at that bright star!" and "I bring this gift for baby Jesus," she said over and over.

"Hush!" Lucy said. "Rehearsal hasn't really started."

"Oh, dordi," Bel said, whirling and twirling all round the stage in a dance all her own.

"In your places, please," Miss Wells said and Polly as Mary slipped out in front of the green curtains and John as Angel Gabriel climbed on a chair behind the curtains and shone his torch down on Mary.

"Hail, Mary," he said in a quavery voice. "Hail, Mary, I have a message for you."

But Mary didn't wait to hear Gabriel's message. She just said, "I feel sick." Then she ran and Mrs Price, who was helping, ran after her.

"Oh, poor Mary!" Miss Wells said. "Oh, poor Polly!"

"Oh, dordi!" Bel said.

There was silence for a moment and then Miss Wells said calmly, "Lucy, perhaps you'd be Mary for today's rehearsal?"

"Yes, please," Lucy said. She felt sorry for Polly because they had been best friends since the infants, but she couldn't help being pleased to be Mary even if it was just for today.

Fortunately Polly had left her doll in the manger under some straw. So that Tuesday afternoon Lucy was Mary and Sharon and Tom and Bel were shepherds and Bel said the right words in the right places and she said "Oh, dordi" a few times too and Adil and Femi and Garry were kings and Kevin was the innkeeper and everybody else was an angel.

"The rehearsal went quite well considering," Miss Wells said when they got to the end and everybody had sung *Away in a Manger*. "Don't forget it's the proper dress rehearsal tomorrow and the big day with the Lord Mayor coming and parents too on Thursday. And by the way if any of you would like to come carol-singing with me on Saturday, ask at home and let me know."

"Me, me, me," nearly everybody said.

"What about the tummy-bug?" Sharon said.

"Hush!" Miss Wells whispered. "Don't let it hear you or it might get above itself."

Afterwards Lucy and Bel walked home.

"How old is your brother?" Lucy said as

they got to the gap in the tall hedge. It would be great to have a brother like Reuben and travel about all the time and never stop anywhere long. Even if it did mean you had to go to lots of different schools like Bel.

"Don't know," Bel shrugged. "About twelve."

"Twelve?" Lucy said. "But your Pa lets him drive the lorry?"

"Our Reuby never drives no lorry. Course not. Don't want no trouble with no gavvers."

"What's 'gavvers'?" Lucy asked.

"Police, course," Bel said.

Rover got up and stretched himself as Bel walked across to the trailer but didn't bark. It was getting colder and there was a blanket over his box now.

"Hello, Ma," Bel said, opening the trailer door.

Lucy went in through the back door. "Hi, Mum. Hi, twins."

"Hello, Lucy," Mum said. She was sitting by the phone and she looked worried.

"Wanna biscuit," Danny said.

"Biscuit?" Davy said.

"There's a trailer next door," Mum said. "I saw it when I went to Tesco's. Gypsies camping, bold as brass."

"Biscuit, biscuit," the twins chanted.

"I know," Lucy said, going pink and trying to make her voice sound ordinary. "Bel goes to my school and her Ma's expecting a baby so they've come for the hospital. She's second shepherd in our Christmas play and guess what, Polly's got the tummy-bug and I was Mary for today."

"Good for you, but poor little Polly," Mum said. "You'd better wash your hands soon as you come in, can't be too careful with the twins having colds."

"OK, OK," Lucy said.

"Well . . . travelling children have to go to school, I suppose, but they can't just stop next door. It's trespassing. I thought of saying something but they've got this dog."

"Rover," Lucy said.

"I was just going to phone Mr Tolley."

"Please don't," Lucy said. "Bel's in the Christmas play and the Lord Mayor's coming on Thursday and Gypsies have come all the way from India hundreds of years ago, and thousands of years ago our great-great-grannies and grandads were

Celts and came over from Europe, especially us because our granny is Scottish and Scots are Celts."

"I wish I knew what you're talking about," Mum said. "Well, we'll have to see what Dad says about Gypsies camping next door."

Chapter Five

Wednesday morning was cold. Lucy shivered and turned up her anorak collar as she walked round to the plot and stood in the gap. The tall hedge was the same but it didn't seem like their old garden any more with washing spread on bushes and a bucket full of empty tins by the trailer door. It didn't seem to belong to Mr Tolley either. It belonged to the Gypsies now.

How long would they stay, Lucy wondered. Mum had told Dad of course and Lucy had told him about the Christmas play and Bel being second shepherd. Dad had frowned and said Gypsies camping next door wasn't on and he'd have to *do* something. When Lucy went to bed Dad and Mum were still talking.

"I won't do anything about the Gypsies until after your Christmas play, Lucy," Dad had said at breakfast. Did that mean they could camp on the plot until Friday, Lucy wondered. She was just going to ask when Danny upset his milk, which upset Mum, and Davy dropped his toast finger on the carpet butter-side down, and Dad left for work.

Outside, Lucy took two steps towards the trailer and Rover jumped out barking.

"Shut it," Ma Lovell shouted, opening

the trailer door. Her fierce black eyes fixed on Lucy. "What ye want?"

"Bel," Lucy stammered. "For school."

A moment later Bel jumped down with her hair neatly plaited again and they set off along the pavement.

"Will ye be Mary again today?" Bel asked, skipping along.

"Might be," Lucy said carefully. "But Polly might get better quickly." She looked the other way as they passed Polly's house. She couldn't help hoping Polly wouldn't be better just yet.

Kate and Don were back that Wednesday morning, but they both looked pale. Miss Wells said they could both be shepherds with Bel and Tom for the moment as Sharon was away with the you-know-what.

"That's four shepherds," Kylie said. "How come we've got four shepherds?"

"Never mind," Miss Wells said. "We need a few spares, don't we? We'll see how things go."

"Polly isn't back yet," Jack said. "I reckon we need two Josephs and two Marys and two innkeepers as well as four or five shepherds and kings."

"Look, it's snowing," Lucy said and everybody looked at the window where fat white flakes were drifting down. By play-time the playground was under a snowy blanket. Rehearsal started early.

Lucy knew Mary's words, she had known them even before the first rehearsal. "Hail Gabriel," and "I can ride the donkey," and "Is this Bethlehem?" and "I need a rest, Joseph." Mrs Budd came to watch the dress rehearsal and after the final *Away in a Manger* she said the play was Very Good and she was sure it would be even better when the Lord Mayor came tomorrow.

It was still snowing when Lucy and Bel set out for home and snowflakes fell against their faces like cold moths and they laughed and ran along the pavement.

But when they got to the plot, the trailer had gone. Snow covered the ground and dark tracks led out to the pavement.

"Ma!" Bel wailed. "Where she to? Where she to?"

"Don't cry, please don't cry," Lucy said. Her own eyes felt all prickly. "They'll come back. They can't be far."

But Bel stood there howling and wailing at the darkening sky. She didn't often cry, not when she burnt her hand on the fry-pan last week, not when Reuby slapped her for nothing, not even when Grandma died three months ago. But Ma and the trailer gone was like falling into a great black hole.

Bel howled.

But suddenly she remembered the *sticks* and she stopped crying and ran to the hard standing and searched for crossed sticks which would show which way the trailer had gone. But all she could see was flat, white snow.

She ran out to the pavement. There was a low wall on the pavement side of the hedge. Sometimes Pa left chalk marks on fences or gates for Uncle Isaac or Uncle Elvis to follow. But there was nothing on the wall except a layer of snow.

Bel cried some more. Tears rivered down her cheeks. People were going home early because of the snow; passers-by glanced at Bel but nobody stopped.

"Want to come to my house?" Lucy said slowly. "You're my second-best friend, aren't you? And my mum'll know what to do ... like dial 999 or something?"

But Bel shook her head, scattering tears like rain.

"That's 'gavvers'. Don't want no gavvers," she howled. "Not in no house." She was used to schools but she had never been in a house in her life. "Course not."

She fixed her eyes on the tracks the lorry had made across the plot, but the pavement snow was flattened by feet and the gutter was grey with slush. She couldn't even tell from the tracks if the lorry had turned left or right.

Suddenly Reuben was there.

"Where ye been, ye little varmint?" he shouted and Bel turned towards his voice. He was coming along the pavement, his cowboy hat all speckled with snow, and everything was all right.

"School," Bel wiped her eyes on her sleeve. "Got back and ye was gone."

"School," Reuben said scornfully. "School don't learn us Gypsies nothing. Put they sticks for ye, didn't I?" He stamped up and down the hard standing, uncovering two crossed sticks which pointed to the right. "Look 'ere! That's what ye got to read, girl."

"Didn't see 'em." Bel sniffed.

"She didn't know where you'd gone," Lucy said.

"What ye talkin' about?" Reuben said,

looking at her for the first time. He frowned and his dark eyes were not friendly.

"Where's Ma?" Bel said.

"'Ospital," Reuben said. "Pains in her belly, baby's starting. Pa took her in the lorry, took trailer too."

"Has the baby come?"

"Course not. Takes a long time, babies getting borned," Reuben said. "Pa says to fetch ye. What ye look like, stray cat?"

He flattened Bel's hair with his fingers and pulled up her hood. "Come on then."

He nodded at Lucy, put his arm round his sister's neck and steered her towards the pavement.

"Goodbye," Lucy called. "Don't forget the play tomorrow, will you?" But neither Reuben nor Bel turned round. Had they even heard? She watched as the two of them disappeared along the busy pavement. An elder brother all your own would be good, she thought, much better than little brothers who scribbled and screamed and spilt things. She opened the back door.

"All right, Lucy?" Mum said. "I was a bit worried with this snow."

"Trailer's gone," Lucy said breathlessly. "Bel's ma is having her baby."

"Thank goodness," Mum said. "Long as they don't come back here. I daresay Dad can fix something across the gap so they can't."

"But that's not fair," Lucy said. "They got to go somewhere."

"They haven't got to camp on the plot next to us," said Mum.

Bel and Reuben scurried along the pavement. They took a street to the left, then right and right again but Bel didn't really notice after that. She wasn't coming back. Gypsies went on and on round the world, they didn't go back. Snowflakes fell against their faces. Footsteps were muffled and traffic moved slowly, wheels slushing along gutters.

"Oh, dordi!" Bel said, looking up at the lights above their heads. Red and green and yellow Christmas lights which flashed on and off making moving pictures. A candle flamed, died and flamed again, bells swung left and then right, Father Christmas winked one eye and his voice said, "Ho-ho-ho."

"Oh, dordi, dordi!" Bel said again, her dark eyes wide.

"School?" Reuben scolded. "Ye silly git,

ye. Travellers don't need no school. Pa and Ma never went to no school."

"School dinner's all right," Bel said. "Christmas play's all right."

"Ye just play all day," Reuben said scornfully. "While Pa and me work, getting scrap and looking after ye."

As they crossed the next street Bel saw high railings and a car park and a big white building behind.

"'Ospital, innit? Trailer's over there." Reuben jerked his thumb. Bel saw the trailer with its silvery pattern and snow on the roof. Her home. She smiled and felt the warmth spread through her.

"Rover there?" she said as they scurried past the trailer towards the hospital building.

"Course. In his box," Reuben said.

"Where's Ma?"

"In the 'ospital," Reuben said. "Come on," he added as Bel shrank back. Going into school was all right but Bel had only been in a hospital once, when Grandma was ill. She remembered that. Grandma, brown as an acorn, lying on the bed like a fallen tree. Grandma dying and afterwards her caravan burnt in the Gypsy way.

Reuben pushed through the swing doors and Bel followed, blinking in the bright light. People were coming and going. Just inside the doors was a Christmas tree with white lights which flashed on and off like tiny stars and presents wrapped in red paper and a doll with a gold wand and wings.

"Stop 'ere, Bel," Reuben said, pushing her towards a line of plastic chairs where people were waiting.

"I want Ma," Bel said but Reuben walked away with a bit of swagger for this strange place and disappeared through another swing door and down a corridor. Bel curled herself up, small as she could.

"You all right, duck?" somebody said. Bel nodded. People passed, people in white coats, nurses in blue, trolleys with tea urns. Names were called and one by one people left the chairs and didn't come back. Bel closed her eyes.

"Ho-ho-ho." Bel's eyes shot open. She had seen pictures of Father Christmas with his white beard and red robe and now he was there in front of her. "Ho-ho-ho, little girl," he said in a creaky old voice. "What's your name?"

"Bel," Bel whispered.

"Bel, eh?" Father Christmas said. "And have you been a good girl, Bel?"

"Course," she whispered as Father Christmas swung his sack to the ground.

"And what have I got in my sack?"

Bel jumped up. They put birds and rabbits in sacks and took them away and they never came back. Bel ran.

"Reuby?" she yelled, pushing through the doors where he had gone and down the corridor.

"Hey," somebody shouted. "Don't run please."

"Stop! Where you going?"

But Bel ran on. Faster. And round the corner and crash.

"What's up?" Pa said. Bel had crashed right into Pa.

Reuben scowled. "What ye doing running about, showing yer ignorance? Told ye to sit still, didn't I?''

"Where's Ma?" Bel stammered.

"Come on back to the trailer, Bel-girl," Pa said. "Babies take a long time acoming. Yer Ma's right as rain."

Chapter Six

It was cold. Under the trailer Rover whined and scratched, he had fidgeted all night. Stopping in a hospital car park was more restless and noisier than the plot. Ambulances came and went ringing bells all through the night and occasionally a car came and went too. In the trailer nobody had slept well.

Bel was snuggled under a warm blanket but she put out one hand to twitch the red curtain aside. From her bunk she could see the yellow squares of the hospital windows and she watched as they began to go out one by one. It was daylight now but the sky was grey and snow covered the car park. Pa and Reuben had got up already and gone across to the hospital. She could see their foot-prints, dark in the white, stretching from the trailer to the hospital doors like a long string of beads.

Had the baby come yet, Bel wondered. Which window was near to Ma?

It was Thursday, the day of the Christmas play at Crossroads School. But Bel didn't think about that. The trailer had moved on and Bel's thoughts moved on too. 'Never look back,' Pa said, 'look forward.' Gypsies had to follow the sun round the earth for ever. Travellers must travel.

She ought to get up. Pa had already lit the

gas stove for her. Bel stared up at the wedding photos and the two steel bowls each hanging on its own hook, one kept for washing clothes, the other for cups and plates. In a Gypsy family the two must never be mixed up and they never were.

Bel jumped up and dived for the shower at the end of the trailer. Twenty minutes later she was dressed and the table set with bread and red plum jam for breakfast.

"No baby yet," Pa said, coming back across the car park with Reuben beside him. "Breakfast ready?"

"Ma all right?" Bel said.

"Right as rain," Pa said, sitting down at the table. "Give 'er a good breakfast, they nurses, I will say that for 'em. Egg and sausage and such."

Bel poured the tea carefully.

"Good girl," Pa said. "Ye got to get to the shops, Ma says."

"What, me?" Bel said and her eyes widened. She always went to the shops but she went with Ma. "All by meself?"

"Come with ye later," Reuben said.

"Where ye to?" Bel said.

"Off out, getting scrap," Pa said. "Ye can come if ye want, Bel-girl."

Bel shook her head. Collecting scrap metal round town and selling it was man's work, "calling" for jumble and making paper flowers and selling them was woman's work. Shopping and cooking and cleaning the trailer was woman's work too. Outside, the car park was filling up with cars.

"Look out for the old dog then, keep 'im quiet," Pa said and he and Reuben jumped from the trailer. "And don't tell nobody yer name nor nothing."

"Course not," Bel said as Pa slammed the trailer door.

She washed up the cups and plates. Then she broke up bread and mixed it with the tin of dog meat and went out to feed Rover. It was very cold and Rover was shivering.

"Poor old dog," Bel said. "Can't let ye off yer chain 'ere, can I?" But she fetched an old cardigan from Ma's sack of jumble and put it in Rover's box. "Good old dog." She waited while he golloped his food and then unhooked him and ran across the car park to the gate and then up and down the pavement. Rover's legs were stiff with cold and at first he limped.

"Don't bark, course not," she said as she hooked him to the trailer wheel again.

After that she cleaned the trailer like Ma always did, plumping the red satin cushions and dusting everywhere, keeping the trailer spotless. She even dusted the Crown Derby china and the cut glass bowls which Ma never let her touch. She dusted the television too. They didn't watch it much, only when they stopped at a site with a hook up to the electric. Then they watched it all night long.

The holly was finished, Ma had sold the last of it. Bel sat down to make paper flowers. Ma never wasted time. Time was money, Ma said. But she was good at making flowers, clever with the pink and yellow tissue paper. Grandma had been even better. Practice makes perfect, she said, her fingers tweaking and pinching like chickens pecking. But Bel wasn't good at flowers and she didn't like being on her own. Hated it.

Halfway through the morning Rover barked.

"Shut it," Bel shouted and thumped the trailer floor. Silence for a moment and then somebody tapped on the door.

"Gavvers?" Bel whispered and knelt behind the red curtains, still half-closed, and peeped out. The house girl, Lucy, was standing there in her grey school uniform. Bel blinked and opened the door, smiling with relief. "Want to come in?"

"Please," Lucy said. She was out of breath and her face was bright pink.

"Get in quick then," Bel said and Lucy scuttled up the steps.

"You stopping here now?" she said, looking round at the shining red cushions and the bright china. The bucket kept for tins was empty now. Fancy living in a trailer, going where you liked, stopping where you liked, free as birds, Lucy thought.

"Course," Bel said. "How did ye know?"

"Reuben said about the hospital. Has the baby come yet?"

Bel shook her head and frowned. "What ye want? What ye come for?"

"Well..." Lucy said and then in a rush she said, "Because it's the Christmas play today with the Lord Mayor and everybody coming and Sharon and Tom and Femi have got the tummy-bug and somebody's got to be king instead of Femi and Polly isn't back yet so I'm going to be Mary and poor Miss Wells is doing her nut and she said, 'Where's Bel?' and I said, 'Shall I go and fetch her?' but I don't think she heard, well I said it very quietly, so I just slipped out playtime to fetch you back."

"Can't come back," Bel said. She looked at the paper flowers and the packet of tissue paper and then she looked at Lucy's eager face and blue eyes. "Can't leave the trailer."

"Why not? Trailer won't run away by itself and anyway Rover'll look after it."

"Don't want to be in no play, do I?" Bel muttered, frowning.

Suddenly Rover was barking again and jumping on his chain.

"Shut it," Bel whispered and she crouched down. "Don't let 'un see ye." Lucy crouched down too and Bel crawled under the table. Somebody knocked at the trailer window.

"Hello!" a man's voice said. "Is anybody there?"

"Gavvers!" Bel whispered. Rover was still jumping and barking. A man's face pressed close to the end window out of Rover's reach.

"It's just an ordinary man," Lucy whispered. "Not police or anything. Maybe he just wants to ask you something?"

The man cupped his hands on either side of his face and peered in.

"I can see you in there, you girls," he said. "Open the door, will you?"

"Better open it," Lucy whispered. "Before he gets cross?"

Bel hesitated a moment and then scrambled out. "Shut it," she shouted at Rover still barking.

"Ah!" the man said as Bel opened the trailer door. "Good girl!" He wore a dark blue suit which looked like a uniform. He wasn't a policeman but he was *somebody*.

"What ye want?" Bel said, scowling.

"What's your name?" the man asked. He had a small notebook in his hand.

"Minty," Bel said. "Minty Smith. Born in a mint-field, wasn't I?"

"Oh-ah," the man said, writing something in his notebook. "And what are you doing here, Minty Smith?"

"Nothing," Bel said.

"Where's your mum and dad?"

"Don't know," Bel said.

"Where have you come from then?"

"Can't remember," Bel said.

"Where you going to?"

"Don't know," Bel said. "Don't know nothing."

"Is your mum in the hospital?"

Bel opened her mouth and shut it again. She didn't know what to say.

The man sighed. "Well, tell your dad you can't stop here, OK?" He snapped his notebook shut and glanced at Lucy. "You look like a sensible girl. Tell 'em they can't stop here, will you? It's not allowed. It's against hospital rules."

"But that's not fair," Lucy stammered. "They got to go somewhere."

"Somewhere else," the man said as he walked away. "Right?"

"That's mean," Lucy said as Bel shut the trailer door.

"Can't stop nowhere," Bel said. "My Uncle Isaac bought 'is bit of land for 'isself. But they don't let 'im stop on it."

"Why not?" Lucy said. "Anyway what you going to do?"

Bel shrugged. "Got to stop 'ere. Can't do nothing else."

"Well . . . well, Don and Kate came back and got sick again and Polly isn't back and you're my second-best friend and I'd really like you to come to Crossroads School and be second shepherd when I'm Mary," Lucy said. "Won't you please come?"

Bel thought of the green curtains and everybody watching and saying she was good and clapping and suddenly she smiled.

"Course," she said.

Chapter Seven

Afterwards Lucy thought that the Thursday when she was Mary and went to fetch Bel for the play was the best day of her life. Well, you needed a second-best friend just in case your best friend wasn't there. She took Bel's hand and they ran through the slippery white streets and got to Crossroads School all out of breath. Everybody in Miss Wells' class shouted "Hurray! Bel's back!" and Miss Wells said "Excellent. Glad to see you, Bel."

"That's only one shepherd, what about the others?" Kylie said, but the buzzer went for dinner just then and Miss Wells didn't hear. Lucy and Bel went to the hall with the others and had pizza and cauliflower and red jelly and custard.

It was too cold to go out after dinner and besides everybody was busy taking chairs into the hall and putting them in tidy rows ready for the Lord Mayor and the rest of the audience.

Bel went behind the green curtains. Everybody was very excited and some people were saying their words over and over in case they forgot. Now Bel was at school she didn't think about Ma and the baby and the man who said they couldn't stop in the hospital car park. She just thought about being second shepherd.

"Who's first shepherd?" Bel asked, because Don and Kate weren't there and Adil was a king now and nobody seemed to know. Bel was second shepherd but there didn't seem to be a first shepherd or a third one either.

"Time to get dressed everybody," Miss Wells said and her voice was all high and breathless as if she was excited too.

The angels put on their white nighties and silver wings and everybody else got into back-to-front dressing-gowns and tea-cloths.

Lucy looked out between the green curtains.

"I can see my mum and the twins," she whispered. She was pleased because Mum had said they might not get there because of the colds.

"Where?" Bel said.

"There," Lucy said, pointing at the twins side by side in the double buggy.

"Kushti," Bel whispered and her smile was sweet as honey. Just as if they were *her* little brothers, Lucy thought.

"Do you think so?" Lucy whispered, looking at the twins again. Sometimes she forgot how small they were and how funny and sweet they could be. She would try and remember. Sometimes. All the chairs in the hall were full now except for one at the front. But the Lord Mayor still hadn't come.

"Oh dear, I hope she hasn't forgotten," Mrs Budd said, looking fussed. Fortunately the Lord Mayor arrived a few minutes later and hurried in.

"Couldn't find the car keys," she whispered as she sat down.

"She's wearing a dress!" Jack whispered. "How can the Lord Mayor be a lady?" Lots of other people were surprised too.

Then the lights went out and the hall was quiet. Mary slipped out between the green curtains and Angel Gabriel stood on a chair just behind the curtains and shone a torch on her.

"Hail, Mary," he said.

"Hail, Gabriel," Mary said.

"You are going to have a baby quite soon," Gabriel said.

"Oh, good!" Mary said and as she was Lucy too, she thought about the twins and how tiny and red they had been when she first saw them.

"Curtains, Paul and Saul?" Miss Wells whispered and the green curtains opened.

Joseph led the donkey on to the stage and

that day the donkey didn't jump about and kick at all.

Joseph said, "We must go and pay our taxes now, Mary."

Mary said, "I'll ride the donkey."

She got on the donkey and they walked up and down the stage for a bit and just for a moment Lucy felt as if she really was Mary. Then she said, "Is this Bethlehem? I need a rest," and they knocked on the door of the inn and the innkeeper took them to the stable. Actually Polly's doll was already in the manger but the audience couldn't see it because it was covered with straw.

Then everybody sang, *While Shepherds Watched* and Bel sang it too. "Just like a little nightingale," Mrs Price, who was playing the piano, said afterwards. Then Paul and Saul closed the curtains.

But Adil was looking worried. "Miss . . . Miss . . ." he whispered. "We got three kings but we only got one shepherd now." But everybody was jumping about and the audience was chattering and Miss Wells didn't seem to hear Adil.

"Curtains," she whispered.

"Don't matter, course not," Bel whispered and as the curtains opened again she walked out on to the stage.

"I'm shepherd one," she said and curtseyed. "Look at that bright star!" she said and then she walked across the stage and ran round the back very fast and came on again.

"Now I'm shepherd two, course I am," she said. "Look at that bright star!" and she danced across the stage, whirling and twirling like a leaf and ran round the back grabbing a shepherd crook with a hook.

"Last shepherd," she said in a crusty old voice leaning on the crook. "Look at that bright star!" She hobbled across the stage and suddenly said, "Oh, dordi!"

She had just seen Reuben sitting in the back row.

Then the curtains closed and when they opened again, the audience could see the baby Jesus doll lying on top of the straw. And Bel, who was still three shepherds, walked across to the stable carrying three gifts, a bunch of cherries, a feathery bird and a packet of jelly babies.

"This is a gift," she said. "And this is a gift and this is the other gift."

"Kushti," Mary whispered, looking at the baby Jesus, and again just for a moment she felt something wonderful was happening and she had changed into Mary from two thousand years ago. But the feeling didn't last long.

Then the kings, Adil and Garry and Jordan, came on wearing their gold crowns and bringing their gifts and then everybody sang *Away in a Manger*. The Lord Mayor sang it too and so did the audience and Mrs Budd. After that everybody clapped and the Lord Mayor said she had been to a Christmas play at a different school every day for two weeks but Crossroads School was the liveliest she'd seen, especially shepherd one, two and three and everybody laughed and clapped.

"That's you, Bel," Lucy whispered.

"Course," said Bel.

After that everybody got dressed in their school clothes again. Mum pushed the buggy with the twins behind the stage.

"Very nice, Lucy, dear," she said. "You made a lovely Mary but I'd better get the boys home now before they fall asleep. They were so excited I had to bring them, colds and all. By the way I'm afraid Danny got hold of Kushti Rosabel's pink dress and washed it and the pink came out rather."

"Doesn't matter," Lucy said in her Mary voice. "Never mind."

Mum looked surprised. "See you later."

"I'm a big boy now," Danny said as Mum pushed the buggy through the door.

"While I think of it," Miss Wells said. "Who's coming carol-singing with me on Saturday?"

"Me, me, me."

"If you haven't asked your parents, be sure to ask tonight and let me know tomorrow. Who's this then?'' she added as Reuben came back-stage.

"Gypsy boy, eh?'' John said.

"Who ye calling Gypsy?'' Reuben said and he scowled like Bel scowled, only worse. He hated being inside, he liked the sky above his head.

"He's Bel's brother, Reuby, isn't he, Bel?'' Lucy said and smiled but Reuben went on scowling and his eyes were black and bright as beetles.

"Where do you go to school, Reuby?'' Miss Wells asked.

"What, me?'' Reuben said. "Ain't got no time for school.'' He looked scornfully at the three Kings. "Plays and that's kid stuff, innit? Ready, Bel-girl, Pa said to fetch ye.''

"Baby come yet?'' Bel said.

"Not yet,'' Reuben said, turning her

anorak right way round and patting at her hair.

Lucy watched them walk away across the playground with Reuben pulling up Bel's hood. It would be really wicked to have a brother like that, she thought.

"Shall I take the baby Jesus doll to Polly's house?" she said. "See if Polly's coming carol-singing on Saturday?"

"Thank you, Lucy," said Miss Wells.

Chapter Eight

It was getting dark when Bel and Reuben left Crossroads School. The rush hour had started early because of the snow, cars revving and people hurrying along icy pavements. Christmas lights hung above their heads and a street away from the hospital they could hear a dog barking.

"Rover?" Reuben said, and they started to run. The old dog barking meant something was wrong. The hospital car park was brightly lit. Rover jumped and barked on the end of his chain.

Then they saw Pa.

He was standing with his back to the trailer door, talking to two men in dark blue uniform. One was the man who had knocked on the trailer that morning.

"What you mean *go!*" Pa shouted, and his fists clenched against his sides like trapped animals and Rover barked louder. Pa had a hot temper, got into fights. Only Ma could cool him down and Ma wasn't there. "Ain't nowhere us can go."

"Well you can't stop here," the man said.

"A car park is for parking cars," the second man said.

"Just doing our job. Says on the notice over there," the man pointed. " 'No Camping.' Can't you read?"

"No," shouted Pa. "No."

"Don't you get funny with me, mate."

"My wife's in 'ospital and I'm not going nowhere," Pa shouted and his fists shot up.

"Pa!" shouted Bel and Reuben, diving forward. Each grabbed one arm and clung on. "Don't!"

The men stepped back.

"You're not doing yourself no good," they said as they moved off. "We'll be back, don't you worry."

Pa watched them go.

"Get in." He jerked his head to the trailer and shook his two arms free. Reuben and Bel jumped inside quick as they could. "Get in and stop in." Pa slammed the door shut and walked off.

"Where's 'e to?" Bel whispered as he

reached the gates and disappeared along the pavement. "Can we go in and see Ma?"

"No," Reuben said. "Pa said stop 'ere, didn't 'e? So we got to stop 'ere."

"Where's 'e to?" Bel whispered, peering into the darkness. "Will 'e come back?"

"Course," Reuben said, squaring his shoulders, the man of the family for the moment. "Better get the kettle on, Bel."

Bel made tea and they drank two cups each, sweet and thick with condensed milk.

"Didn't get to no shops," Bel said. "But there's baked beans?"

"Better not," Reuben whispered huskily. "Better wait."

It was nine o'clock when Pa came back with a newspaper parcel full of fish and chips all warm. He was all right again now, spreading the paper and smiling as they dipped the chips in tomato sauce.

"Better get some sleep." He crumpled the paper in a ball.

"What about the baby?" Bel whispered.

"No baby yet," Pa said.

They were eating breakfast next morning when a nurse tapped on the trailer window as she passed.

"Baby's come," she called.

"Boy or girl?" Pa shouted after her, flinging back the trailer door, but the nurse had already reached the pavement and didn't hear.

Bel grabbed her anorak and Reuben grabbed his cowboy hat and they followed Pa, running across the snow and in through the swing doors.

"Don't run. Walk please," somebody said.

Ma was sitting up against her pillows. There was a cot at the end of her bed.

"Ma!" Bel cried, running across the ward and flinging herself into her open arms. She hadn't seen Ma since Tuesday. Bel had never been away from Ma before for three whole days. "Oh, Ma!"

"Oh, dordi, my Bel," Ma said, folding her arms round her. "Oh dordi, dordi!"

"All right?" Pa said. "Boy or girl?"

"Boy, innit?" Ma said, glancing at the cot. "Course 'e is."

"Boy," Pa said, touching the baby's fingers. "Lovely little boy. Treat ye right, they nurses?"

"Course," Ma said. "Right as rain."

"What we call 'im?" Reuben asked.

"Joseph?" Bel said, looking down at her little brother. "Kushti, right kushti. Can we call 'im Christmas?"

"You barmy or what?" Reuben said. "Can't call a baby *Christmas*."

"Liberty," Pa said. "After his Grandpa."

"Liberty Joseph," Ma said. "Get 'im christened June up at Appleby?"

"Right," Pa said.

"Can I 'old 'im?" Bel said.

"Ye'll only wake 'im up," Ma said.

"Ye kids better get back to the trailer," Pa said. "Ma needs a bit of peace and quiet."

Reuben and Bel kissed Ma and walked back along the corridor. Father Christmas was standing in the hall with his sack on his back.

"Ho-ho-ho! New baby is it?" he said.

"Boy," Bel said. "My brother, Liberty Joseph Lovell."

"That's nice," Father Christmas said. "You been a good girl, Bel?"

"Course," Bel said. She wasn't frightened of Father Christmas any more, not with Reuben right beside her and a new baby brother, not after being three shepherds in the Christmas play at Crossroads School.

"Like a present from my sack?"

"Course," Bel said. "A present for my baby brother like a teddy bear."

"Blue for a boy?" Father Christmas put down his sack and rummaged inside. "This one all right?"

"Excellent," said Bel.

That Friday was the last day of term at

Crossroads School. There was lots of tidying up to be done and everyone in Miss Wells' class was talking about the Christmas play. Every time the classroom door opened Lucy hoped it would be Bel but she half-knew already that Bel wouldn't come to school any more.

She wrote in her news book about the trailer arriving in the night on the plot next door and Bel coming to school and then the trailer going to the hospital car park because of the baby.

In the afternoon she drew a picture of the trailer and picked out the silver pattern with real silver paint that Miss Wells found at the back of the cupboard. Then she drew Bel in her red dress standing in front of the trailer and her eyes felt all prickly.

"That's lovely, Lucy," Miss Wells said.

"But is something the matter? You do seem rather quiet."

"Bel won't be back now, will she?" Lucy said. "Because Gypsies never stay anywhere long and she's my friend, my second-best friend, but I shan't ever see her again and I didn't even say goodbye."

Mrs Price came and Miss Wells went out and came back a bit later.

"I just phoned the hospital," she said. "Mrs Lovell has had her baby. It's a little boy."

"Hurray!" everybody in the classroom shouted.

"I'm going to see the baby after school," Kylie said. "Might take a present."

"So am I," Kate and Charlene said.

"And me, and me," said several others.

"I don't think that's a very good idea,"

Miss Wells said, "because Mrs Lovell will be very tired. But we're going carol-singing tomorrow, so why don't we meet in the hospital car park a bit early, say three o'clock? You can bring something for the baby if you like, and say goodbye to Bel. Ask your mums if that's all right, will you?"

"Yes!" everybody shouted and just after that Lucy had the postcard idea.

Chapter Nine

"The trailer's over there," Lucy said, pointing. The snow across the car park looked dirty now.

It was three o'clock on Saturday afternoon and thirteen children from Crossroads School followed Miss Wells across to the hospital main doors. Lucy, Kylie, Ben, Saul, Femi, Kate, Charlene, Polly, Kevin, Jack, Jordan, Adil and Sue.

"Looks like the tummy-bug is over, no new cases since Thursday," Miss Wells said, and she was right.

"Hurray!" everybody shouted.

"I didn't get it," Ben said.

"Neither did I," said Lucy and Kylie.

Some children had brought gifts for the baby. Kylie had a packet of chocolate money, Ben had a rattle bought with his own pocket money, Polly had a blue baby blanket, Kate had a baby tee-shirt and Lucy had two woolly hats the twins had grown out of and a postcard stamped and addressed to herself for Bel. Miss Wells had a box with baby soap and talc.

"I'm afraid we can't all go in," Miss Wells said. "Fifteen visitors all at once would be too much for Mrs Lovell, not to mention the other mothers and babies. So I suggest Lucy and Ben and me take the gifts inside and you stand outside and sing

While Shepherds Watched and *Away in a Manger* in your best voices, so all the mothers and babies in the ward can hear."

"But it's cold outside," Femi said.

"And that's not fair," Kylie said.

"Look," Polly said, pointing. "It says only three visitors on the notice board."

Lucy collected up all the gifts in a plastic bag and Kylie sighed and dropped her chocolate money in. "Don't you dare go eating it."

"Course not," Lucy said.

"Which is Mrs Lovell's window?" Miss Wells asked.

"Ground floor, Bel said, third one along," Lucy said, pointing. "That one."

"Oh yes. Mother and Baby Unit. Get ready then," Miss Wells said as the children gathered under the window. "Adil, you'd better start them off."

"We're like the three kings or the three shepherds," Lucy whispered as she and Ben and Miss Wells pushed in through the swing doors. Lucy had only seen Mrs Lovell once or twice and she felt rather shy as they walked into the ward. Fortunately Bel was already there.

"Hello, Bel," Miss Wells said. "Good afternoon, Mrs Lovell. Congratulations. What a lovely little baby boy! I'm out carol-singing with the children from Crossroads School. You'll hear them outside in a minute. We've brought one or two things for the baby."

"That's nice," Mrs Lovell said, looking in the bag. She had a shawl round her shoulders. "Bless ye, lady."

"I bought the rattle for him with my own

pocket money," Ben said.

"Bless ye, me deary. Bless the lot of 'em," she added as the children struck up *While Shepherds Watched* outside. Two other mothers in dressing-gowns moved across to look out.

Lucy looked into the cot. The baby was red and wrinkled but not so red and wrinkled as the twins had been.

"Isn't he sweet?" she said politely and Bel smiled.

"Liberty-boy," she said, pushing one finger into his little fist. "Ever so strong, 'e is. Real Gypsy boy, 'e is."

"Where's Reuby?" Lucy whispered.

"Gone out, getting scrap with Pa," Bel said.

"See this postcard," Lucy said, pulling it out of her pocket.

"Kushti," Bel said, looking at the picture of daisies.

"It's for you to write and send to me later on."

"What for?" Bel said.

"Because you're my second-best friend," Lucy said. "And I put a stamp and the address on it. So all *you've* got to do is write a message when you stop for a bit somewhere. Promise?"

"Gypsies never stop anywhere long," Bel said.

Outside, a ragged second verse of *While Shepherds Watched* died away.

"Little angels," somebody murmured. Suddenly a loud clattering came from the car park. Bel ran to the window.

"Lorry with a big hook," she screamed. " 'E's taking our trailer."

"What lorry? What ye on about?" Ma shouted.

Outside eleven carol-singers stopped singing and stared, and inside two carol-singers, Lucy and Ben, ran down the corridor as fast as they could with Bel as well. Miss Wells followed more slowly.

Outside Kevin said, "What you doing?"

"What's it look like?" The driver of the lorry jumped from the cab. "Towing off this trailer."

"Yours is it?" his mate said, jumping down the other side.

"Course not. Belongs to the travellers," Kevin said.

"You can't do that," Charlene said. "It's not fair."

"Only doing our job," the driver said. "Only doing what they told us."

"They haven't got anywhere else to go," Adil said as Bel and Lucy and Ben came running out through the swing doors.

"How can they find a place to stop in the dark?" Polly said.

"That's their problem. Off you go, you lot," the driver said.

"Hang on," his mate said. "Christmas is Christmas. I got kids of my own."

"You going soft or what? Out the way, kids."

"No," Kevin said. "No, no, no."

"No, no, no," said the other twelve carol-singers from Crossroads School and Bel. And they all joined hands like a daisy chain and spread right round the trailer.

"*Away in a Manger*, that's what we got to sing," Kevin said. "Only doing what she told us."

"*Away in a manger...*" the carol-singers began and the singing was much louder now and dozens of faces were watching from the hospital windows.

"Let's get out of 'ere," the driver said. "Nobody never said nothing about a bunch of kids."

"*The stars in the bright sky...*" the carol-singers sang as the two men climbed back into the lorry and drove off.

"Never heard *Away in a Manger* so well sung," Miss Wells said, coming out through the swing doors of the hospital, and inside the mother and baby ward everybody was clapping.

When the carol was finished Father Christmas came out.

"Ho-ho-ho," he said. "Are you all good children?"

"Course," they shouted, and he gave each one a balloon.

"Happy Christmas," he said fourteen times.

On Boxing Day Lucy and Dad walked to the hospital in the afternoon. The snow was melting a bit by then and the car park was patched black and white like a piebald pony. The trailer had gone but Lucy could see where it had stood, and follow its track marks up to the road.

"I wonder which way they went?" Lucy said, trying to picture it. "I wonder where they are now?" It was odd having a second-best friend you might never see again, and a bit sad too. "Bel's Uncle Isaac bought his own plot but they won't let him stop on it."

"Planning rules, I expect," Dad said.

"Tough life for travellers, especially this weather."

"Yes," Lucy said. "I might get a postcard from Bel one day." But a voice in her head whispered, "This year, next year, sometime, never."

"Don't hold your breath," Dad said. "But your mum and me are talking about going to Devon this summer, staying in a caravan again."

"Brilliant!" Lucy said. "But what about the twins?"

"I reckon we can manage the twins between us, don't you?" Dad said. "They'll be coming up to three by then."

"And I'll be ten!" Lucy said, imagining six caravans set against a green bank with a hawthorn hedge at the top. She would tell the twins all about it beforehand. It would be wonderful living in a caravan for a fort-night in the summer, but dire in the winter with nowhere to stop. "Same farm?"

"If you like," Dad said. "I'll give them a bell tonight."

"And when it gets warmer, can Polly and me sleep in the garden in the tent again?" Lucy said.

"Don't see why not," Dad said.

School started a week later. Lucy's drawing of the trailer with the real silver paint was still on the classroom wall. Lucy smiled to see it.

"It's all right, that picture," Ben said.

"I wonder where they are now?" Lucy said. "I gave Bel a postcard all stamped and she promised to send it back to me."

"Don't hold your breath," Ben said.

Two weeks later Miss Wells took the drawing down and Lucy took it home. She stuck it on her bedroom wall and looked at it for a long time. Two weeks after that the builders started on Mr Tolley's bungalow and a month after that the grass on the plot began to grow and Lucy found she could put her foot on twelve daisies.

"Look!" she said to Mr Tolley one weekend. "Gypsies say it's spring when you can put your foot on twelve daisies."

"Humph!" Mr Tolley snorted. "And what is it when you can put your foot on twelve empty tins they left behind? Don't talk to me about Gypsies."

"Sorry," Lucy said. "But what are they supposed to do? I mean it's not fair to be cross when they haven't got any proper dustbins or anything."

She had forgotten about the postcard by this time. Almost.

Bel had forgotten about the postcard too. The Lovells were camping in the New Forest with wild ponies grazing round the trailer and everything was green. Pa and Reuby were mending gates and getting scrap and Ma was strawberry-picking. The baby was crawling now and Ma put him in the buggy and Bel had to keep him happy. One evening Ma was cooking the evening meal, rabbit stew and fresh nettles, and Bel found the postcard in her pocket.

"What's this?" she said and gave it to Liberty and he put it in his mouth.

Bel sat on the steps with the sky above her head and a skylark singing. She had been to school in Ringwood for a bit and she would go again after the strawberry-picking. She hadn't thought about Crossroads School since she left but she thought about it now.

She had been scared of house-people back in the winter but she wasn't any more because of being in the Christmas play and because of Lucy. Bel remembered then and took the postcard back and gave Liberty-Joe her old doll instead. When he was bigger she could tell him about India and Egypt and they would both go to school. Now Bel curled her tongue over her upper lip and wrote on the postcard very slowly, "Reuby an me an Liberty-Joe an Ma an Pa ar well and stoppt in th nu foris for storbery pikkin at Fordingbrig which is kushtie. Luv from Bel."

After all, Bel thought, she was Lucy's second-best friend. Two weeks later when they moved on she dropped the card in a red pillarbox. Gypsies never stop anywhere long.

Lucy took the postcard to Crossroads School and for a few minutes everybody was talking about Bel and the Christmas play again. After that Miss Wells put the baby-chewed postcard on the noticeboard in the hall for the whole school to see.

And as far as I know it's still there.